Curious George®

Rain or Shine

Adaptation by Erica Zappy
Based on the TV series teleplay written by Chuck Tately

SCHOLASTIC INC.
New York Toronto London Auckland
Sydney Mexico City New Delhi Hong Kong

ISBN 978-0-545-36098-2

17   16/0

Printed in the U.S.A.   40

First Scholastic printing, April 2011

Design by Afsoon Razavi

Curious George was a playful little monkey. Like most playful little monkeys, he loved having fun outside.

But sometimes the weather would not cooperate with George. It would be too windy for playing ball. Or too wet for flying a kite.

George was tired of the weather ruining his fun. He decided that he would just have to be prepared for anything.

Then the doorman told him that some animals have a special way to tell the weather. George was curious. He didn't think that he was one of those animals, but maybe he could become one!

George decided to ask his friend the man with the yellow hat. The man told George about a saying that sailors use to help them predict the weather: "Red sky at night, sailor's delight." This meant that if a sailor saw a bright red sunset, the next day should be sunny!

That gave George an idea. He would draw pictures of the sky and then watch what happened to the weather. He started with the red sunset that evening.

The next day was warm and sunny.
He drew a picture of that below the sunset
from the day before. He even drew the cricket
he met while he was drawing. Chirrp! Chirrp!

The next morning there were dark clouds to draw. His cricket friend was back, but he was much quieter on that chilly day: Chirrp. By that afternoon, it was raining.

Hmm . . . did clouds mean that it would rain? George thought so. These drawings were becoming very useful!

The next day George used his drawings to help make a decision. When the man asked if George wanted to go on a picnic, George predicted that the clouds he saw that morning would mean rain later on. He decided to stay at home.

But it never rained! In fact, it was a beautiful day. The blue sky was full of fluffy white clouds.

Ah-ha! So maybe dark clouds meant that it would rain! White clouds meant the weather would be good. George was so happy when he saw a sky full of white clouds the next morning. Now he could go on that picnic.

But George's happiness did not last long. Wind blew a storm in that soaked his sandwich. The wind had ruined his picnic, and his prediction. This weather business was not easy. How was George supposed to predict wind too?

The next day, George noticed a flag flapping in the wind. He didn't have a flag, so he used the man's sock as one. George watched as the sock flapped in the direction the wind blew.

George also had a pinwheel. When the wind blew fast, his bee pinwheel spun quickly. When the wind blew slowly or not at all, the pinwheel spun slowly too. Now he could tell how fast the wind was blowing.

As a special treat, George's friend took him to the weather station for a visit. There were no socks, pinwheels, crayons, or crickets. How did they predict the weather? The weather scientists told George that they used radar and satellites in space to find weather patterns.

Unfortunately, they were missing one of their satellites. They wouldn't be able to predict the day's weather for the mayor's big golf game. George had an idea!

George raced home. The sock and pinwheel showed the morning's storm clouds were being blown away. His drawings showed the sky was red the night before, and the cricket was chirping quickly. George predicted it would be a good day for golfing! He could predict the weather after all!

Back at the weather station, the mayor was happy to hear the news! He invited everyone to come to the golf course.

George had one more prediction to make that day—tomorrow would be a great day for a picnic!

Making Your Own Weather Journal

Curious George was able to help the weather scientists, or meteorologists, by using the information he kept in his weather journal. You can make your own weather journal, and you can even use some of the same things George used—like a pinwheel, an old sock, and maybe a cricket, if you can hear one nearby!

In your journal, you can draw pictures of the colors you see in the sky and different clouds you see in the morning, in the afternoon, and at night.

You can collect rain outside and measure it. Rain you collect in a day is the daily rainfall. You can measure for the week and the month, too. Just use an old container and a ruler.

In the winter, you can collect snowflakes using black construction paper and a magnifying glass. Draw them in your journal. No two are alike!

Make your own tornado!

Luckily a tornado didn't come ruin George's picnic! Tornados can form from clouds in a thunderstorm and can have very high winds.

What you need:
(Please get a grownup to help you with this project.)

- Two 2-liter soda bottles
- Water
- Food coloring and glitter
- One 1-inch washer (available at a hardware store)
- Duct tape

What you need to do:

1. Fill one bottle with water. A little more than halfway is best—don't fill it to the top.

2. Put in a few drops of food coloring and glitter, if you are using any.

3. Place the washer on the opening of the bottle with water in it. Put the second bottle on top of the first so that both bottle openings touch with the washer between them.

4. Duct tape them together securely to prevent leaking!

5. Turn the bottle so the one with water is on top. Give a circle-shaped twist to the bottle and a tornado will form in the water as it drains into the bottom bottle!

George learns a lot about the weather by watching clouds. Did you know there are many different kinds of clouds? Here are the four most common kinds:

Stratus: clouds that look like big blankets of white in the sky—from a word that means "layers." They might bring rain!

Cumulus: the big, puffy clouds that look like piles of cotton balls—from a word that means "heap." Usually cumulus clouds mean good weather—picnic weather!

Cirrus: clouds that are high and wispy—from a word that means "hair." They are made of ice crystals and can mean bad weather.

Nimbus: clouds that produce rain—from a word that means "rain." These are usually big and might be gray!